DAWN PATROL

orca sports

DAWN PATROL

JEFF ROSS

ORCA BOOK PUBLISHERS

Library and Archives Canada Cataloguing in Publication

Ross, Jeff, 1973-
Dawn patrol/ Jeff Ross.
(Orca sports)

Issued in print and electronic formats.
ISBN 978-4598-0062-5 (pbk.).—ISBN 978-1-4598-0063-2 (pdf).—
ISBN 978-1-4598-0064-9 (epub)

I. Title. II. Series: Orca sports
PS8635.06928D39 2012   jc813'.6   c2011-907771-x

First published in the United States, 2012
Library of Congress Control Number: 2011943730

Summary: When their surfer friend Kevin disappears in Panama,
Luca and Esme risk more than just big waves to find him.

*Orca Book Publishers is dedicated to preserving the environment and has
printed this book on Forest Stewardship Council® certified paper.*

Orca Book Publishers gratefully acknowledges the support for its publishing
programs provided by the following agencies: the Government of Canada
through the Canada Book Fund and the Canada Council for the Arts, and the
Province of British Columbia through the BC Arts Council and
the Book Publishing Tax Credit.

Cover photography by Getty Images
Author photo by Simon Bell

ORCA BOOK PUBLISHERS
www.orcabook.com

Printed and bound in Canada.

20 19 18 17 • 5 4 3 2

For CB, we'll always have Panama.
And to the rest of the December 2010 crew—
thanks, it was a blast.

chapter one

The waves were coming in perfect sets of three. It had taken Esme and me four hours on a sixteen-foot water taxi to get here. The boat bobbed on the edge of the swell. We watched a dozen surfers paddling to get in position. Now that we had made it to Bocas del Mar, an island off the coast of Panama, the bumpy boat ride was worth it.

"Do you see him?" Esme asked.

We scanned the lineup of surfers for our friend Kevin Taylor. He had left Los Angeles in March. It was now June, and other than the email he sent before he split, we had heard nothing from him. The email wasn't much help:

Guys,

I need to get out of here. Nothing is making sense at the moment. I don't know if I'll come back, but if I don't, know that I love you both. Esme with all my heart, and Luca in a totally best-bud, non-romantic way.

Kevin

Esme and I knew how nothing made sense to Kevin. In January his parents had died in a plane crash near Bocas del Mar. Kevin's father was an experienced small-plane pilot. The morning of the crash, a dense fog patch caused him to fly into the side of a mountain. It took two days for anyone to reach the crash site. No bodies were found. But, given the state of the plane's destruction, that wasn't surprising.

Kevin had spent many Christmas vacations in Panama with his family. He had traveled all over the world following waves with his father, a fanatical surfer. Kevin was an amazing surfer too. He was always searching for larger and larger waves. He liked what people called unrideable breaks, the kind of waves an average surfer wouldn't even attempt.

Which is why we had come to Bocas. According to surfline.com, the center for all wave-related surfing information, a giant swell was coming toward Bocas. Most big waves form out in the Pacific Ocean, breaking in Tahiti or along Hawaii's north shore. But this monster was coming toward Panama. It was still two days out, so for now, the waves were in the five-to-seven-foot range. By all accounts, forty- or fifty-foot waves were approaching. If Kevin was nearby, he would be here to ride them.

Esme was somewhat familiar with Panama. While she had never been to Bocas del Mar, she had been to several of the surrounding smaller islands with Kevin's family two years before. Esme and Kevin had been dating for three years, and I had known him since we were kids. With his parents gone, we were the closest thing he had to family. Esme's father, a high-flying banker, often had business meetings in Panama City. Esme's dad knew how much Kevin meant to us and that we were worried about him. When Esme asked if we could go to Panama to see if Kevin was there, her dad was happy to fly us down with him after our final exams. He said it would be a business trip for him and a grad present for us. We spent a few days in Panama City together before he put us on the water taxi.

"These surfers all look alike," I said to Esme.

She screwed her face up and punched my shoulder. "They do not. You, for instance, are a surfer but look more like, I don't know, a scientist or a violinist."

"A violinist?" I said. "What does a violinist even look like?"

"Like you," she said, laughing.

I was almost six feet tall and had shaggy brown hair. My skin had gone a darker shade than it likely should have from all the time I spent in the sun. I didn't know what violinists looked like, but I had a feeling they didn't spend 80 percent of their waking hours in surf shorts and a reef shirt.

"These are beautiful waves," Esme said.

When Esme was a kid, she was a tomboy. She was the kind of girl who could kick your ass at any sport. Then she grew up and became a gorgeous girl who could still kick my ass at any sport, including surfing. Unfortunately, she bailed heavily last summer, so now she's cautious when it comes to any wave over eight or nine feet.

The boat captain shouted, "You stay here?"

"Sí," I called back, using my entire Spanish vocabulary.

"On island?"

"Sí."

"I take bags in," he said. He pointed at a large hut on stilts above the water. "Leave them with Delgado, sí?"

"Delgado?"

"Sí. It is only place to stay. For tourists."

5

Before I could answer, the captain revved the boat's engine and gunned across the shallow reef. He threw our backpacks onto the dock and took us back out to the break.

Esme tossed her board into the water and dove in. I followed.

The captain leaned over the side of the boat. "I will come back?"

"Three days?" I asked.

"Three days." He pointed at the dock. "Delgado's." And with that, he tore off.

"Think we'll ever see him again?" Esme said as she climbed onto her board.

I watched the boat become a dot on the horizon. "I hope so." I lay on my board and paddled toward the small gathering of surfers along the edge of the break. "But for now, let's catch some of these waves."

I looked over the edge of my board, and there was nothing but sand.

A girl sitting on a long board outside the break waited her turn.

"Hey, do you speak English?" I asked.

She smiled at me. "Um, yeah. How about you?" Her blond hair glistened in the bright sunlight.

"A little," I said. "Is this a sand bottom the whole way in?" Esme paddled up beside me, and the girl stopped smiling.

"No. Farther in it's reef. Be careful. If you get over near those rocks, it's really shallow." She pointed toward a cluster of rocks that jutted out of the ocean.

"Cool, thanks," I said. "By the way, my name's Luca and this is Esme."

"Alana," the girl said before she lay down and paddled into a wave. She rode the crest for a moment, then dropped down onto the other side.

"Not bad," I said.

Esme looked at me. "What do you mean, Alana or her surfing skills?"

I must have blushed, because Esme said, "Yeah, I thought so."

"Am I not allowed to...?"

She punched me on the shoulder again. "You're not allowed to sit here talking about girls when there is a perfect wave coming in and you're next in line." The wave was a roller, gaining height and speed as it approached. "Go, go, go," she said.

I paddled hard and lined myself up for the first ride of the day.

chapter two

You have to catch a wave at just the right time. If you try to stand up too early, you sink. Stand up too late, and you get bowled over by the wave and dumped down the front side. When to stand up is not really something you can be taught. You have to feel it.

I paddled as hard as I could. Still, by the time it was upon me, I only had a moment to push down on the board and stand. I managed to get up and glided along the top of the wave. I pushed forward, dropped down the front of the wave, kicked out and shot sideways. Even though the wave wasn't tall enough to have a full-sized barrel, I got a nice ride out of it. Better surfers, like Kevin, would have slid along the crest. Maybe even spun or launched off the top. For me, it was enough to feel the awesomeness of all that water moving beneath me, to be a part of something that had crept in from the middle of the ocean.

I kicked out again, rolled over the backside of the wave and slid down onto the board. I could see a dark line of coral four feet beneath me. I paddled outside the breaking waves and joined the lineup again. The wave I had caught was the last in a set. Everyone bobbed around on their boards looking at the horizon, waiting for the next one.

I paddled over to Esme and sat up on my board.

"That was nice," she said.

"Thanks. There's a reef up there. So the waves get bigger and bigger as you go in."

I pointed to the other surfers. "You ask anyone about Kevin yet?"

"No. But I seem to have their attention." Esme was in a bikini. A very small bikini. She had a reef shirt on, but it was white and did little to discourage glances from the lineup.

"Hey, guys," I said. Most of the guys looked at me as though they only just realized I was there. "We're looking for a friend of ours. Tall, with curly blond hair, rides a red Piranha board?" The three guys closest to us all tilted their heads slightly before unleashing a flurry of Spanish.

"Sorry," I said. "I only speak English."

"We be here today," one guy said. He pointed at his friends. "No one. Just us."

"Okay, thanks," I said.

The guy shifted a little closer to me. "Girlfriend?" he said, nodding at Esme. He flicked his eyebrows at her.

"What?" Esme said.

"He wants to know if you're my girlfriend," I said.

The guy winked at her. "Very beautiful. Like flower."

11

Now it was Esme's turn to blush. "Come on," she said. "Let's cut over." There was another handful of surfers bobbing around on the other side of the swell.

"You don't want to stay here and chat with these nice gentlemen?"

I could feel another punch coming, so I lay down and started paddling. As we neared the other side of the break, the next set came roaring in. The waves seemed bigger, rising as they pushed inland.

"Faster. Move it!" Esme yelled from behind me.

It is no fun to be swept over by a big wave. I paddled as hard as I could, turned into the wave and duck-dived through it. A duck dive is a simple move to get from the front of a wave to the back without shooting to the crest and being flung backward. You simply push down on the front of your board and dive into the face of the wave.

I came out the other side, and Esme popped up a moment later. One surfer had grabbed the wave. Alana and another surfer watched as he cut back and forth, bellowing as he went.

"Hello again," I said to Alana as we paddled up to them.

"Long time no see," she said.

I noticed she had an American accent. The other surfer looked like a local. He squinted at us, propping a hand over his eyes to block out the sun.

"A friend of ours might be here. We're not sure." I described Kevin to Alana.

"Can't say I've seen anyone like that," she said. "But maybe give it a day, right? With those monster waves coming in, every surfer worth his salt will be here soon."

"Sure," I said. "What about him? Does he speak English?"

"I don't know." She looked at the other surfer and spoke to him in Spanish. The local shook his head, never taking his eyes off Esme and me. He was in his mid-twenties and had dark-brown eyes. His hair was cut short on the sides, giving him a strange faux-hawk. He was sinewy, yet, like a lot of surfers, muscular.

"He says no," Alana said.

"No to English, or no to seeing our friend?"

"Both," Alana said.

"Our friend's name is Kevin. Kevin Taylor."

"Kevin Taylor?" Alana said to the local.

He shook his head again and paddled into a small wave. He got up on his board but had to pump hard to move across the wave.

"Looks like you guys freaked him out," Alana said. "Are you staying at Loco Delgado's?"

"Loco?" I said. "I hadn't heard the Loco part before."

Alana laughed. "Yeah, well, that was his name back in the day. I don't think he's really crazy. Anyway, unless you want to sleep on the beach or grab a water taxi back to the mainland, Loco Delgado's is your only choice."

"Back in what day?" I asked.

"Word is, Delgado used to wander the world looking for giant waves. I don't know how much of it is true. People seem to make up fascinating stories about themselves around here."

"Well, our packs are there," I said.

"Cool. If anyone knows about your friend, it will be old Loco. He's completely dialed into everything that happens here." Another set was roaring in, and Alana quickly paddled toward where the wave would crest. "See you in there. Catch the right wave and you can ride all the way to the beach." The wave boiled under her. She worked her arms around like pinwheels. Then she shot down the face of what must have been a nine-foot wave. It was the biggest I had seen yet.

"Nice," Esme said.

"Alana or her riding?" I said, leaning away from her.

"Shut up and grab the next one," Esme said. "Let's get in to shore and have a chat with old Loco Delgado."

chapter three

Delgado's hotel was a cluster of huts. Some of the huts were on the beach or in the jungle. The rest were on stilts above the ocean, at the end of warped piers. Esme and I managed to ride almost all the way to shore. I cut to the right on the wave I took, and Esme cut to the left, which sent her toward the large black rocks. I watched her bail, well before she came in too close, and swim out of the maul of the next breaking wave.

"It's like the waves want to wreck you on those rocks," she said as we dragged our boards onto the beach.

"Or they just want you to cut to the right," I said. We walked along the beach until we came to a pier leading to the hotel's office. The office was a thatch-roof hut, only slightly larger than the surrounding huts. The only way we could tell it was the office was on account of a large OFFICE sign pegged near the entrance.

Reggae was playing inside. The music had a soft, light beat, and for the first time since we had arrived in Panama, it wasn't Bob Marley. We lay our boards beside our backpacks and went inside.

A big white guy was lying on a couch with a MacBook on his stomach. He swiveled his head toward the doorway.

"Hola," he said.

"Hey," I said. "Are you, um, Delgado?"

"Loco Delgado," he said. He set the laptop on the ground and rolled off the couch. His T-shirt clung to him. Other than a small fan, which seemed to be doing little

17

more than pulling the heat in from outside, there was no air circulation. It smelled musty, as if the room itself was sweating. Delgado was our parents' age, although his skin was wrinkled and leathery from too much time in the sun. I tried to imagine him touring the world searching out the best waves. But his rotund form didn't seem to fit the mold. "Are you the two Armadio brought over earlier?"

"Yeah," I said. "We need a place to stay for a couple of days. Do you have any vacancies?"

Delgado nodded his head seriously and walked over to the counter. He ran a finger down a blank page, then looked up at us. "I think you can be accommodated," he said, laughing.

"There's no one else here?" Esme asked.

"Sure, sure. I think there are about twenty people here right now. They'll let me know when they decide to check out. And pay as well."

"That's very trusting of you," I said.

Delgado rolled his head from shoulder to shoulder, and a succession of cracks and pops sounded. "Surfing is a culture. You know how it is, man? What you give is what you get. Nice waves come in, and people feel good. The last thing they want to do is rip someone off and start feeling bad." He leaned back to look out the window. "There's an empty hut right here. Has a double in it. I imagine one bed will suffice?"

"Actually, two would be better," I said.

Delgado nodded. "That's all right. The double is actually just two singles jammed together with a big mattress on top. We can pull them apart." Delgado came around the counter. "Come on, I'll show you your new digs."

"Wait a second," Esme said when we were outside. She opened the front pocket on her backpack and pulled out a photograph of Kevin. "Have you seen this guy?" She handed the picture to Delgado.

He glanced at it and handed it back. "No. Why?"

"He disappeared a couple of months back. We're trying to find him," Esme said.

"What makes you think he would be here?" Delgado asked.

"In January his parents died in an airplane accident on one of the nearby islands."

Delgado nodded. "I remember," he said. "It was a stormy, foggy day. I remember because it was clear first thing in the morning, and then a fog set in and the waves got angry. They were mean that day. Out for blood, some of the locals said."

Esme and I stared at a colorful school of fish in the water off the pier. Esme cast her eyes down, but I could see they were glazed. Kevin's parents were kind, giving people, and Esme was the daughter they never had. She spent more time at Kevin's house than anywhere else. It was still hard for us to believe his parents were gone. Kevin's family had always made me feel like family. A heaviness settled on my chest, and I gulped a couple of times to hold back tears.

Delgado reached down and grabbed my backpack. "Let me show you the hut. How many days do you think you'll be here?"

Esme's damp hair hung across her face. She was working hard at not crying.

"Until we find him," I said.

The hut had two stories. The first was an open space with a barbecue and some chairs. The upper level had a bed, sink, compostable toilet and a giant window facing the water. The sun was starting to set, and a dim orange glow filled the upper level.

"Ahh, it's nice in here," Delgado said. "I like this hut. It's one of my favorites." He looked at me. "Oh, man, I almost forgot. The single mattresses are in another hut. Do you want to help me get them?"

"It's okay," Esme said. She pulled her sleeping bag out of her backpack and tossed it on the bed. "This will work."

"You sure?" I said.

"Sure." She went and sat on the bed with her back to us.

"All right," Delgado said. "Stay as long as you like, pay when you leave. Respect everyone and everything around here, that's all I ask. The jungle, the beach, the waves, one another. Be kind." He reached out and shook my hand. "And if you need anything, I'll be next door." He pointed out the window. From where we were, we could see right into his hut. "There are two restaurants along the beach. But, and I say this as an honorary local, I wouldn't go much beyond the Purple Parrot."

"Why?" I asked.

"This island has its locals. When big waves come in, the island really fills up with surfers and, well, the locals get a little testy."

"I can imagine," I said.

"Fair enough, right? You wouldn't want a bunch of tourists invading your backyard either. So stick to this end of the island, and you'll be fine."

The smell of barbecuing shrimp wafted in the window, and my stomach growled.

"Is that smell coming from the Purple Parrot?" I said.

"Special on garlic shrimp tonight." Delgado smiled again and shuffled out of the hut.

"He's not here, Luca," Esme said without turning around. "We're never going to find him."

I clasped her shoulders. I could feel her trembling. "He'll be here, Esme. He might not be here yet, but he will be."

She shook her head. "How can you know that?"

I didn't. I didn't have a clue where Kevin was. He could be in Australia for all I knew. But I had to believe the lure of these big waves would be enough to deliver him to us. And I needed Esme to believe it too.

"I don't know. But we have to hope, right?" I said.

"I guess."

"You know it." I squeezed her shoulders. "Let's go get some dinner. I'm starved."

chapter four

We slept soundly and awoke well rested. The tide rolled in and out beneath our hut. I turned over to find Esme staring at me.

"You snore," she said.

"I do not."

"You are the last person who would know it, Luca. So I'm here to tell you, as the only person who has ever shared your bed, you snore."

"You're not the only person I've ever shared a bed with."

She grinned. "I'm not, am I? Do tell."

"I'll have you know my cousin Jeremy and I used to camp out all the time. And when I went to San Francisco with Kevin last year, we shared a bed." At the mention of Kevin's name, we both fell silent. Esme rolled out of her sleeping bag and picked up a sweatshirt off the floor. She walked to the window and gazed at the ocean.

"I guess we missed dawn patrol," she said.

The best waves of the day are often during the early morning tide. Any surfer who rises to catch them is part of what is called the dawn patrol. There's something mystical about being out in the ocean as the sun is rising. It's peaceful and different from any other time of day. It feels as though everything is starting over again.

I slipped out of my sleeping bag and pulled on a pair of shorts. "Yeah, I guess we did."

"If Kevin's here, he would have already been out surfing."

I opened my backpack and retrieved a breakfast bar. I had eaten a hundred of these since leaving LA. They weren't getting any better. "By now he'd be back in bed dreaming of giant waves. Speaking of which, what are the waves like?" I went and stood beside her.

"Still coming in pretty nice. There are people out on both breaks."

I could smell fish cooking somewhere. Birds were calling to one another in the jungle, and the mist from the ocean was fresh and cool on my face.

"Want to get some breakfast or head straight out?"

"Let's go out. I'm not hungry."

The waves were rolling in. Four or five waves would come in and break, and then there was an interval of calm. Fish swam beneath our boards, and during one lull I saw a turtle. The waves were a reasonable height, six or seven feet, and curled nicely when they broke. I took the first good wave, rode it out and then sat on my board to watch Esme. She dropped into a seven-foot wave and rode in the barrel, white foam lapping above her. She got ahead of the wave, shot out the end of the barrel and launched herself up and over the backside.

"Very nice," I said when she paddled over to me.

"These are beautiful." She grinned.

I was relieved to see her happy. As we paddled back toward the break, I saw the surfer from the day before who hadn't wanted to speak to us. He was bobbing in the middle of a pack of surfers.

"There's that guy from yesterday," I said. "Think he'll try to avoid us again?"

"I don't think he was trying to avoid us," Esme said. "It seemed to be more of a language issue."

"I'm not so sure," I said. He hadn't seemed freaked out by a couple of gringos. He seemed as if he wanted to get away from us. "But, whatever. Let's go talk to them."

Another set came in. The break shifted slightly to the left. We duck-dived through each wave. By the time we got out to the break, there was only one surfer there.

"Well, hello again," Alana said.

"Fancy meeting you out here," I said. A couple of surfers paddled toward the shore. "Where did everyone go?"

"They cut to the other break," Alana said. "It's bigger over there now."

"These are good waves here," I said.

"Exactly, and now everyone is gone," Alana said.

"Hey, did I see that guy from yesterday out here?" I said.

"Yeah, he was here. His name is Jose. He's been out all morning."

"Where does he hang out?"

Alana raised her eyebrow, then glanced at Esme. "Umm, aren't you two together?"

I looked at Esme and caught on to what Alana was getting at. "No, we're not," I said. "Nor would I be interested in getting together in, um, that way with this Jose guy. I just wanted to try and talk to him about our friend."

"Your friend," Alana said. Another set came in, and we lay on our boards in case they got bigger. "Right. Still haven't seen him."

"Did Jose go to the other break?" I asked.

"Yeah," Alana said. "He always goes where the biggest waves are. Or at least that's what he tells me."

There seemed to be another swell coming in. Alana sat up on her board.

"How about we cross over," she said. "I was going to stay here for a bit, but there's no harm in seeing what the other side is like." She paddled into a wave. "Watch out for the rocks when you get over there. People get mashed on them all the..."

"What?" I yelled, but she was already on a wave, riding the crest before dropping down the front. I turned to Esme. "What did she just say?"

"Don't get killed," Esme said.

"Ahh, good advice."

"Your wave," she said, pointing at the next cresting mass.

I lay down on my board and started paddling. "See you over there."

chapter five

I caught the next wave and found the sweet spot, the place where you can feel the water rolling perfectly beneath the board. The board feels weightless, and all you have to do is stand up as quickly and smoothly as possible.

I dropped down the front of the wave. It wasn't curling very well, but it was big and solid enough to keep me moving toward the beach. I carved up and down the front of it, cutting back and forth across the face.

I spotted the giant black rocks on the reef closer to shore. The wave started breaking behind me, losing its momentum. Soon it would wear out and slink in to shore. I cut hard across the top of the wave and lay down on my board, but the wave carried me toward the rocks. Alana was ahead of me, paddling through the surf. I paddled toward her and immediately hit rock. When the water rose, I quickly paddled away.

As I reached the other side of the reef, another wave came in. I duck-dived through it and watched it smash on the rocks. The pull of the ocean yanked me backward, and I paddled hard into the next wave and ended up over the reef again. Alana was cutting across the incoming waves, duck-diving as she went. I tried to follow her, but each wave pushed me farther back. I was used to five- or six-foot waves, and I had never been in such a strong riptide. It actually did seem as if the water wanted to smash me into the rocks.

Eventually I got outside the break and was able to paddle up beside Alana. "That is not easy," I said.

"Yeah, I followed a local across the reef yesterday when I first arrived, and it was tough. If those big swells come in, no one will be making that cut."

"You only got here yesterday?"

"I got to the island the night before and was in the water first thing yesterday morning."

So Kevin could be here but just hadn't been out surfing. I spotted Esme paddling toward us. The waves had died down. The black rocks glistened in the sun.

"Wow, that's really shallow," Esme said.

Another set of waves, larger than the last ones, crashed in. "You got out of there just in time," Alana said.

"Did that Jose guy already catch a wave in?" Esme asked.

I looked at the line of surfers. They were all facing out to sea, watching the approaching waves, waiting for the perfect one. "No, he's right there," I said.

Jose was lying on his board. He started paddling, preparing to take a wave. He looked our way. It seemed as if he was staring right at me, so I waved. Then the wave rose up, and he disappeared.

"I'm taking the next one," I said. "Maybe I can paddle in with him, take him to Delgado's and show him Kevin's picture."

I paddled into the next wave and caught it at the last second. I was about to drop down the face of the wave and cut away from the giant black rocks when a surfer came out of nowhere. He headed directly at me. I had two choices, smash into him and go under, or ride the wave out in the opposite direction and try to avoid the rocks. I looked back to see who had cut me off. Jose carved to the tip of the wave, then drove back down. I thought he had taken the first wave. What was he doing out here? Why would he wait for another wave when he had a perfect one? And why did he cut me off? He had to have seen me.

I didn't have time to think about it. I had to concentrate on staying on my board. The wave was messy. It was big and moving fast, but it was tumbling in on itself at odd points. So instead of being able to ride the wave in, I had to contend with a choppy surface and unpredictable collapsing.

I tried to get high on the wave in order to pop over the back and paddle away from the rocks. But every time I drove up the wave, it fell in on itself and became a mess of frothing water. I was getting closer and closer to the rocks, and the wave seemed to grow larger and larger. I was already over the reef. The wave was pulling all the water off the reef, leaving only a foot or so beneath me. If I fell, I'd be crushed on the coral.

I tried to power my way back up the front of the wave. I even considered jumping up to the top of the wave, hoping I could swim away from the rocks. But as I cut up, I lost my balance, and a second later I was flat on my back, the wave crashing on top of me.

My board shot into the air, and the leash yanked me backward. I sucked in as much air as I could before I went under. When you wipe out, you never know when you will resurface. Sometimes you pop up and have lots of time before the next wave rolls in.

Other times you stay under for a full set of seven or eight waves and come up gasping and choking and thankful to be alive.

I didn't smash into the reef right away. I got boiled into the wave, rose toward the surface and was slammed back down. I put my hands out to brace myself. I touched something briefly, but was pulled away almost as quickly. A second later, I popped to the surface. I took a deep breath and saw I had been driven to the edge of the break. I was still a distance from the rocks, but the next wave would surely push me closer. I tried to dive through the next wave, but my board caught on something and I was yanked backward.

The wave crushed me. I felt as if I was in a washing machine set on high. I rolled over and over. I covered my head with my hands. My hands and feet were thrashed against the reef. It felt as though my skin was being shredded.

I popped up, but couldn't get a full breath. Then I was under again, rolling and flipping, completely at the mercy of the waves.

I opened my eyes and tried to figure out which way was up. Everything around me was swirling and seemed to slow down. It was like being in a slow-motion dream where you can see every bit of light, every grain of sand, every cell of every living thing. I watched sand float like dust in the sunlight and followed its slow trajectory toward the surface. Then I swam as hard as I could toward the sunlight. A moment later, I was coughing and spitting out salt water.

My eyes stung, and my lungs felt as if they were on fire. Another wave was coming in. I grabbed the leash and started pulling the board toward me. The back of the wave pumped me up to the surface. I was right beside the rocks. They glistened in the sun, foam and seaweed sliding down their sides. I managed a single gulp of air before the next wave crashed onto me. I felt as if I was going to be swept in to shore. But then the riptide grabbed me and dragged me out to sea again.

I have no idea how far out I went. The last thing I remember seeing was a big rock in front of me.

After that, everything went black.

chapter six

The sky vibrated. Something smelled like peaches and vanilla. There seemed to be a dozen blurry faces swimming above me. Voices surrounded me, not words, just voices. I tried to turn my head, but it was as if my head was in a vise. I closed my eyes and heard my heart beating. It pounded through my body. I was going to be sick. I opened my eyes, rolled onto my side and threw up.

The voices returned. Louder than before. I could make out two faces above me. One of them was Kevin's!

I tried to speak. But all that came out were bubbles. I rolled onto my side again to spit. When I turned back, the only face I saw was Jose's. He narrowed his eyes, and then a second later he was gone.

I coughed up some more water. I felt as though I had been dragged through the ocean with my mouth open, which wasn't that far from what had happened. I pulled myself up onto my hands and knees. I was certain I had seen Kevin. And Jose. I couldn't have imagined it. But when I looked around, there was just a guy in a pair of dripping surf shorts holding my broken board in front of him. Kevin and Jose were gone.

"Are you all right, dude?" the guy asked. He was blond and tanned, and so muscular it looked as if he had snapped my board in half with his bare hands.

"Who was just here?"

He tilted his head and rapped on one ear, trying to dislodge some water. "What?"

"There was someone here," I said. "Two people."

"Yeah, maybe. A couple of guys dragged you in after you totaled on Old Man."

"Old Man?"

"The rocks out there that you flailed yourself into." He held the two pieces of my board out again. "I got your board for you." He dropped the useless bits of fiberglass at my feet.

I sat down and coughed some more. "What did the guys look like?"

"I didn't see them, brah. I saw you get totaled, and then two dudes dragged you in to shore. I didn't see who. I was on my way out. There was a break in the waves, so I grabbed what was left of your board and brought it in. And now I'm going back out, if you're all right."

"Yeah, yeah, I'm all right." If I was a sunbather who had been smashed by a wave, people would have gathered around to make certain everything was fine. Surfers generally get left on their own.

"Cool," he said and dove back in.

Esme and Alana ran up. "Luca, what happened?" Esme said.

"Jose cut me off."

"What?" Esme asked. "We saw him catch the wave ahead of the one you got on."

"That's what I thought too. But he must have dropped off it and caught the next one. He came out of nowhere and went straight at me."

"That's weird," Alana said. "He didn't strike me as the kind of guy who would try to rub you out on the rocks."

"Well," I said as they helped me stand, "that's what happened. The weird thing is, I swear I saw Kevin. With Jose."

"What?" Esme said.

"When I came to, I swear I saw Kevin standing over me. Everything was foggy. Their faces looked see-through. But I swear I saw him."

"Where did he go?" Esme said, looking up and down the beach.

"I don't know," I said. "The surfer who brought me my board said he saw a couple of guys pull me out of the water. But he didn't get a good look at them."

"Um," Alana said. "You might want to get that looked at." She pointed at my leg. Blood dribbled from a long cut on my shin. "And that," she said, pointing at my shoulder. I put my hand there, and it came away red. "And kind of all over." She looked back at the water. "I'm not going in there for a while. You just sent an open invitation to every shark within fifteen nautical miles."

"Sorry," I said.

She smiled, a really warm smile, and stepped up beside me. "No worries, I was done for the morning anyway." She grabbed my arm and threw it over her shoulder. "How about we get you over to see Delgado."

"Delgado?" I said.

"Yeah, Delgado used to be a doctor or something," Alana said. "He'll patch you right up." Alana and I took three steps together before Esme spoke up.

"You want me to bring what's left of your board?"

I looked at my surfboard. It was broken in two, and bits were missing as well.

"No," I said. "It's toast."

Esme took the two ends and jammed them into the sand so they looked like a couple of headstones. "Rest in pieces," she said.

chapter seven

"A paramedic, actually," Delgado said. He had made room for me on his couch and was digging in a cabinet for a first-aid kit. "What happened?"

"This guy cut me off my wave."

"That doesn't really happen around here. Normally people are very cool about taking turns."

"Do you know a surfer named Jose?" I asked, touching my head gingerly.

There wasn't a cut there, but it was throbbing painfully.

"Jose? What does he look like?"

"Kind of small, dark-brown eyes. Faux-hawk."

"What kind of board?" Delgado asked. "That's normally how I tell who's who."

"Looked like a Channel Islands. I don't know which model."

Delgado put some swabs and cotton balls on the coffee table and handed me an ice pack for my head. He inspected the cut on my shin. "Can't say I do," he said. He looked up at me. "This is not going to feel nice. How are you with a bit of pain?"

"It needs to be cleaned," I said.

"He whimpers and cringes like a child," Esme said.

"I do not."

"Remember that splinter I took out of your foot last week?" She gave me a lopsided grin.

"I just really hate splinters," I said. "That's all."

Delgado dabbed at the cut on my leg with an alcohol-soaked cotton ball. It stung at first, and then it felt as though the alcohol dove deep into my flesh and was grinding away in there. It was all I could do to not grab my leg and scream.

"Yeah," Delgado said, looking up at me. "But I'd say that's the worst of it. It's not really that deep a cut."

"How deep is it?"

"We'll see. Hold still." He went back to work.

I buried my head in the back of the couch to take my mind off the pain. Then someone took my hand and held it tightly. I glanced over, expecting to see Esme, and found Alana kneeling beside the couch. She took the ice pack from me and pressed it to my head.

"Are you sure it wasn't just an accident?" Esme asked.

"A guy pretends to take one wave, jumps on another, then comes out of nowhere and tries to ram me into some rocks? No, I don't think so."

"Maybe he missed the first wave, then pumped for the next one and didn't see you. It happens," Alana said.

I thought about this. It does happen. Sometimes you miss a wave and don't want to give up on a good set, so you catch the next one. There's a chance you might not notice someone on the following wave because you are taking it late. But it seemed as if Jose had wanted to force me into the rocks. As if he was aiming for me.

"Maybe," I said. Delgado did something to my leg. I inhaled quickly.

"What could he have against you?" Alana said. "You've only just met."

"Barely met," I said through clenched teeth.

"You're in luck. It's a surface cut. A bit of liquid skin will do the trick," Delgado said. "Same with the shoulder."

"Liquid skin?" I said.

"It's like a band-aid you spray on. It helps seal the cut, keeps germs and bacteria out, and lets it heal. I don't think you need stitches," Delgado said.

This was a relief. I looked down at my leg and, now that it was clean, could see that what I'd thought was a gash was simply a long, thin scrape down my leg. "Go for it," I said.

"Who knows you're here?" Alana asked.

"No one," I said.

"Well, there's you two and the boat driver," Esme said. "And the surfers that were out yesterday. But they don't really know us. I mean, we're just a couple of tourists to everyone else."

"A couple of tourists who are looking for someone," I said.

"You didn't tell anyone you were coming to Bocas?" Delgado asked. He was applying the liquid skin. It made a hissing sound as he sprayed it on my leg.

"My parents know I'm down here with Esme, and her dad is in Panama City. But we haven't talked to him since we got here," I said.

"It must have been an accident," Delgado said. "This is a very chill spot. I can't see that kind of thing happening here."

He sprayed a few spots on my feet. "You have to keep these covered or you'll have an infection by tomorrow. Wear shoes today."

"You mean you think I can surf again tomorrow?"

"With the size of the waves coming in, I'd guess you'd have to lose a leg before you stayed on shore. Am I right?"

Yeah, I thought and nodded. Pretty much.

The cuts didn't look bad at all once we were out in the sun. Esme had gone to our hut and returned with my Reef shoes. Esme, Alana and I settled down on the beach and watched the surfers.

"Are you here on your own?" Esme asked Alana.

"Yeah. I broke up with my boyfriend in Mexico. We were doing a whole surf-trip thing. Straight down the west coast. But..."

"That didn't work out," Esme said. "Gotcha."

"Yeah, it didn't work out. We hadn't really been dating very long. It was stupid of me to take off with him. But I wanted out of Florida, you know? I wanted to surf some real waves. Anyway, we had planned to come here after Mexico. But he decided to go back up north and find some giant waves. You know, some real monsters, not these crappy little Central American ones."

"If Surfline is right and this place goes off in the next couple of days, then the joke will be on him," I said.

Alana nodded and dug her toes into the sand. "So do you really think Jose tried to ride you into the rocks?"

"Yeah. I really do. It seemed deliberate."

"Well," Alana said, "he's local local."

"Local local?" I asked.

"Like, he lives on this island, not one of the other ones around here."

"What makes you think that?" Esme asked.

"He told me."

"What else is on this island?" I asked.

"There are some huts on the north end. I think there might be some other restaurants and clubs. But they're all for the locals. I was told they're not tourist-friendly."

"But you think Jose might live on the north side of the island?"

"It's possible," Alana said.

"Well, I'm not doing any surfing until I get a new board." I looked at Esme. "Want to go for a little walk?"

Esme stood and wiped sand off her long legs. "Sure," she said. "Why not."

"I'll come too," Alana said. "You know, in case you need some muscle." She flexed a slender arm for us and laughed.

chapter eight

After lunch, Alana, Esme and I walked as far up the beach as we could before ducking onto a trail that we hoped would lead to the north end of the island. Alana led the way, looking over her shoulder now and then to keep the conversation going. The jungle was loud. Birds cawed from trees, and there seemed to be giant crabs everywhere. Each time we took a step or spoke, they scurried into the undergrowth.

"Have you been up here before?" I asked.

"No, like I told you, I just got here the night before you arrived," Alana said.

"So how do you know about the clubs and everything?" Esme asked.

"You didn't hear them last night? It was *whomp, whomp, whomp,* all night long."

Esme and I shook our heads. We had passed out well before a dance club would have started up.

"Did Delgado tell you anything about the village?" I asked.

"Yeah," Alana said. "Not to go." She stopped in front of a tree that had fallen across the trail. "I think the locals feel their island gets overrun by tourists."

"What makes you think that?" I asked.

She put a foot on the tree and hopped over. "Because Delgado told me they felt that way." She laughed. She really had a great laugh.

"So us going up to the north end?" I asked.

Alana reached a hand out and helped me over the log. I did the same for Esme.

"Maybe not the best idea," said Alana. "But it's not like they dislike foreigners.

Delgado said they're just worried about getting run out."

We started walking again. "On another note," I said. "How many different things do you think live in this jungle that could kill us?"

Alana laughed. "More than you want to know."

The village came into view slowly. It was like nothing I had seen before. All the huts were on stilts about five feet off the ground. They were connected by raised board-walks made of different-colored planks. The huts were painted random colors as well. Most of them were made of plywood. None of the windows had screens. And where a portion of a house had fallen away, it was replaced by corrugated steel or bamboo stalks or whatever else washed up on shore.

Music filled the air, and there were people everywhere speaking Spanish.

"Keep an eye out for Jose," I said.

We decided to stay on the main track. No one was unfriendly, but no one was inviting us to dinner either. A wave came in, crashed on the break wall, spilled over and flowed beneath the walkway. People moved slowly in the heat, and dogs barked in the distance.

"I wonder what will happen if the waves that are coming are as big as Surfline says they will be," I said.

"I don't know," Alana said. "The villagers might not even know about it. They aren't exactly hooked into the web, are they."

"They have to know, right?" Esme said.

It seemed as if all that came out of the local radios was reggae. Though maybe every so often there was a quick interruption of news and weather.

A pair of locals approached. We moved to the side to let them pass and were forced onto a second walkway. A woman shouted at us from a nearby hut.

"What did she say?" I asked quietly.

"Umm," Alana said as we stepped back onto the main walkway. "Kind of like, 'Stay off my lawn.'"

"Oh," I said. I suddenly didn't feel safe. The warm glow of a beautiful afternoon faded.

We made it to the northern tip of the island. There was a dance club and a little bar facing the ocean. We ducked into the bar and found a table with a view of the water and the village. The bartender ignored us until Alana got up and ordered three fruit juices from the bar.

"What are we going to do if we find this Jose guy?" Esme asked.

"Just talk to him. There has to be a reason he doesn't want me out surfing," I said.

"But why?" Esme asked.

"I swear I saw Kevin. And Jose was right beside him."

"Come on, Luca. You had just been smacked in the head and nearly drowned," Esme said. "You could have seen angels or gargoyles."

"Yeah, but I didn't. I saw Kevin."

Alana came back with our drinks. She shook her head. "I'm not so sure you want to drink these."

"Why?" I asked.

"This is not really a tourist bar. You know?" Alana said. "More of a locals-only vibe. The bartender cringed at my Spanish."

We stared at our fruit juice. I was thirsty, but I wasn't prepared to drink something that might make me ill.

"She scooped the ice from a different bucket," said Alana. "The juice came out of a plastic container not one of the bottles that were right there. And she only washed her hands after she'd finished making the drinks." We pushed our drinks to the middle of the table. "Plus, I'm pretty sure I was overcharged."

"We'll pay you back," I said.

Alana laid her hand on mine. "No problem, *señor*." She had amazingly green eyes, big and wide. They looked like the water in the depths of a coral garden.

"There he is," Esme said.

I whipped my head around. "What? Who?"

Esme slowly stood. "Jose."

Jose was with two other guys. One of them was pushing a wheelbarrow full of coconuts. I half stood, and he spotted me. Before I could say anything, Jose bolted. He ran off so fast he knocked the coconuts right out of the wheelbarrow.

chapter nine

I was first around the table and out the door. Esme and Alana followed. The walkway was jammed with people. I jumped onto a smaller one to get past them. A flourish of angry Spanish followed my every step.

I spotted Jose on a walkway leading to the eastern side of the island. I skirted around a pair of women, then leaped over a bundle of bamboo stalks lying on the ground. The walkway veered out over the ocean. Beneath me, crabs scurried into hiding.

I slowed down and checked to see if Esme and Alana were following me.

"Did he go this way?" Esme asked when she caught up.

"Yeah," I said. "Where'd Alana go?"

"I don't know. She was right behind me."

"Come on, she'll catch up." We started running again, saying, "Excuse me, excuse me, excuse me" as we passed people.

At the eastern edge of the island, we headed south. The five-foot-high walkway stretched out over deeper water. Ahead, a group of people chatted and drank beer at a wide junction. I slowed down and searched for Jose's face in the crowd. The walkway forked. One section cut back into the jungle, the other continued out over the water. I was about to take the jungle route when I saw Jose slink out from beside a hut. He had his head down and his hands in the pockets of his surfer shorts.

"There he is," I said, pointing. We started running and got within twenty feet of him when a big guy in dark sunglasses ran out of a hut and barreled into us.

I tried to get my balance, but I slipped and fell headfirst into the water. I popped up just in time to see Esme hit the water.

"Are you okay?" I asked.

Esme felt along her leg. A bit of blood hazed the water.

"Yeah, just a scrape from the coral," she said.

I looked up at the walkway. Jose and the big guy had disappeared. A bunch of people were laughing and shaking their heads at us. Someone yelled at us in Spanish. I think it was, "Go back where you came from, gringos."

"Esme, over there," I said, pointing to where the walkway led onto the beach. We swam out past the reef and into deeper water before cutting back to shore.

"Well," Esme said once we were sitting on the beach. "That sucked." She checked her cut knee. It was just a scrape, but coral scrapes were worse than pavement scrapes. Coral reefs are a living organism, like a giant animal. When you're cut, part of the organism stays in the wound and makes it sting more than you could ever imagine a little cut stinging.

"Do you still think Jose is just a local who doesn't like gringos on his island? He recognized us and ran away."

"That's odd," Esme said. "But what would Kevin be doing with someone like Jose? If Kevin is even here."

"He is," I said. "I'm more sure of it now than ever."

"But why would Kevin take off? If he knew we were here, he would come and find us, right? He would..." Esme stopped and touched her cut knee. "He would want to be with us."

I put my hand on her shoulder. "I don't know, Es. Maybe he's in some kind of trouble. If he's here, we'll find him."

She looked at me with watery eyes and a trembling chin. It would be heartbreaking to have come this far to find Kevin, only to have him disappear again.

"We have to go back and find Alana," I said.

"No, you don't." Alana jumped off the end of the walkway. "Alana found herself."

"You're all right?" Esme asked.

"I am. I thought you guys had gone the other way. It took awhile to figure out you came this way. Um, why are you both soaked?"

"Some giant tossed us into the water," I said.

"What?" Alana frowned. "I know Delgado said the locals can be unfriendly, but that unfriendly?"

"Someone doesn't want us to find Kevin," I said.

Alana sat down beside me in the sand. "And so you two are just going to go on home and forget any of this happened?"

"Um, no," I said.

"Yeah, I didn't think so." She bumped me with her shoulder, then stood back up again. "Come on, there has to be a way back to the other side of the island from here. Unless you want to go back through the village."

chapter ten

We were a mile down the beach, our clothes beginning to dry in the warm afternoon sun, when we spotted a tall building still under construction. It looked like a hotel. Not a giant hotel like the ones on the beaches of Miami but a small, two-story hotel. Only half of the windows had been installed. Out front, a long pier, which seemed sturdier than the village walkways, was attached to a large dock with benches, chairs and a slide.

"What's this?" I said.

"I don't know," Alana said. "Looks like a deserted hotel."

We hadn't passed a single hut or person on our way down the beach. The hotel was surrounded by jungle.

"Want to go in?" Esme asked.

"Sure," I said. "Why not?"

Inside, it was cool and dark. The half-finished lobby had a high ceiling and stairways on either side of a bamboo desk.

"Snazzy," Alana said. "This will be a nice place someday." There were tools and supplies jammed in corners, but it didn't look as though anyone had been working on the place for some time.

"It feels abandoned," Esme said. She ran up a set of stairs to the landing and popped her head into each of the doors along the second floor. "The rooms are all empty. Some have, like, bathtubs and sinks and stuff," she called out. She stopped at one door. "This one has a bed."

"Weird," I yelled up to her. I approached an empty windowpane and looked out.

It was a beautiful view. In the distance the surrounding islands were green and black shadows in a sea of blue. Blue waves dotted with whitecaps. A blue sky smudged with clouds. It was a view people would travel great distances and pay lots of money to see.

Alana stood beside me. "This is amazing," she said.

"It is. Why do you think it's not finished?" I asked.

"Who knows."

I spotted a sign off to the side of the property. I went outside to read it. It was written in Spanish and English. The Spanish was in a giant font, while the English looked like an afterthought at the bottom. *Another slice of paradise brought to you by*_____. A piece of cardboard was taped over the last word. I lifted a corner of the cardboard and peeked underneath. I couldn't read the word, but there was something about the font that seemed familiar.

"What's this?" Alana asked.

"It's the developer's sign," I said. I peeled off the tape and removed the cardboard. Beneath it was the word *Fallbrook*.

I dropped the cardboard.

"What?" Alana said.

Esme had come outside. "The back of the hotel goes right into the jungle, and there's a pool with a swim-up bar. Who doesn't like a swim-up bar?" She looked at me. "What?"

I pointed at the sign.

She walked over and stood beside me. "Oh, wow," she said.

"What?" Alana repeated, sounding peeved.

"Fallbrook is Kevin's family's business," I said. "It's his mother's maiden name." We knew Kevin's family was wealthy. They had developed properties all over the world. But we didn't know they owned anything here.

"I thought they'd gone bankrupt," Esme said.

"Really? Your friend's family's business was broke?" said Alana.

"Yeah," I said. "They were being investigated. I don't know what it was all about. Kevin never wanted to talk about it. But it must have been serious. His dad had been selling off properties in California. I knew they had some property in Hawaii and Tahiti, but nothing down here."

"That explains why it looks like construction suddenly stopped," Esme said and shivered.

"So who owns this place now?" Alana asked.

"I don't know," I said. "I guess the bank."

"Let's get out of here. This is kind of creeping me out," Alana said.

"Agreed," I said. We headed down the beach, searching for a path through the jungle to the south end.

"So, if his family was bankrupt, how could your friend afford to take off from LA?" Alana asked.

"Life insurance," I said. "His family had a huge plan. And when both your parents die..." I stopped. I had liked Kevin's parents a lot. You could talk to them about anything and not be lectured or judged. His dad was one of the main reasons I started surfing. They had been good people, and now they were gone.

"Can't you imagine us all staying at that hotel?" Esme said. "The three of us?"

"Yeah," I said. "I can."

Alana jogged ahead a little.

"You think Kevin's here because of the hotel?" Esme asked.

"No," I said, "I think he's here because this was the last place his parents were." It made sense. There was nothing in LA for him. No other family. No one except us.

"Maybe," Esme said. She grabbed my hand and squeezed it. "So why wouldn't he want us to find him?"

I squeezed her hand back. "I don't know. We'll just have to ask him when we find him."

"Hey, guys." Alana had stopped walking. "I think I found a trail."

It looked more like a tunnel through the jungle than a trail. The trees towered above us, and the grass was high on either side. "Do you think it leads back to Delgado's?" I asked.

Alana shrugged. "I guess we'll find out."

chapter eleven

Waves are born of nature—big waves, anyway. A large container ship can create three- or four-foot waves, as will a giant cruise ship. But those kinds of waves are really displaced water. Big waves, waves that come rolling in from out in the middle of the ocean, waves that boil up and gather speed, body and energy—those are waves only nature can create. Man can monitor waves, with the help of technology. Oceanographers can track them and, with some certainty, pinpoint where and when they will reach land. A number of websites post surf reports, forecasts and wave speculation, but the most popular is surfline.com. The predictions on Surfline are eerily accurate—sometimes down to the minute. So when Surfline posted that some big waves were going to break on the shores of Bocas del Mar in the morning, it was accepted as a fact.

So even though Esme and I were intent on finding Kevin, there was no denying our thoughts drifted now and then to images of big waves. The jungle trail had led us to the Purple Parrot. The three of us had dinner while a soft breeze came in off the water. The owner made us feel at home, which was just what we needed after our afternoon at the north end of the island. After dinner, Esme and I dropped Alana off at her hut and returned to our own.

"I agree with you," Esme said and zipped her sleeping bag up. "He has to be here."

"He does," I said.

She rolled over, and I looked out at the moonlit water for a while before I grabbed my own sleeping bag. As I drifted off to sleep, I wondered what the next day would bring us.

I woke once in the night to the rumble of distant thunder. All the other jungle sounds were swallowed up by a steady thrumming. In my drowsiness, I dismissed it and drifted back to sleep.

Esme woke before dawn. I was still dozing when I heard her say, "Dawn patrol, Luca."

The thundering sound was still there. It was as if a busy highway had been erected outside our window overnight. It grew louder and louder as I slowly drifted toward consciousness.

"What?" I said.

She walked toward the window. "Surf's up. The big ones have arrived. Listen to them."

I jumped out of bed and ran to the window. "Are they breaking?"

"They must be," she said. The moon was gone, and the sky was just beginning to lighten. It was still too dark to see the ocean. "I heard Delgado get up awhile ago. There are people over there eating breakfast."

"Let's go," I said. I ran across the room and slipped into my shorts.

"Aren't you forgetting something?" she asked.

"What?"

"You don't have a board."

I pulled my Reef shirt over my head. "I'm hoping Delgado has one to loan me."

Delgado did not have a board to loan me. He did, however, have a variety of boards for rent for twenty-two dollars a day, which was steep. Giant waves, fifty or sixty feet high, were about to be rolling up to these shores. To be without a board would be criminal.

I chose a short board with straps, in case I needed to be towed into the waves.

There are a few different ways to surf. The traditional method is to paddle hard into the wave when it approaches and then pop up on your board. Then there's tow-in surfing, which is completely different and relatively new. Trying to get on a wave over forty feet high using the traditional paddle method is impossible. You can't get enough speed going to enter the wave. So, a number of years ago, some surfers started being towed behind a Jet Ski and dropping into waves.

It isn't often you see a surfer cutting left or right along the line of a big wave. Instead, you drop in and shoot straight ahead, pushing to get out of the way of the crest before it drops down on you. It's similar to snowboarding in an avalanche. In a big wave there is a massive force collapsing behind you, waiting to eat you whole. Your only shot at survival is to stay on your board, no matter what.

When daylight broke, we were on the beach staring out at the break.

"Those have to be twenty feet high," Esme said. I checked that the liquid skin on my leg was holding up. I couldn't feel the scratches and cuts on my feet—though at that moment, with my adrenaline pumping, I didn't feel much of anything.

Delgado was on the dock getting his Jet Ski ready. "They are almost here," Delgado yelled. "You want to go out?"

"Um, yeah!" I yelled.

Delgado had a trailer hooked to the back of the Jet Ski. I laid my board down on it, and Esme did the same. I didn't see Alana anywhere. I figured she would be out soon, at least to watch.

We hopped on the back of the Jet Ski behind Delgado. I let Esme get on first, then balanced myself between the trailer and the ski. Delgado followed the shoreline until he found a way out past the breakers. As we drew closer, the waves seemed even larger and more beautiful. They rolled past where we had been surfing the day before. The black rocks sunk beneath the water with each surge.

"I don't think you need to tow into these," Delgado said. We bobbed outside the break. No one had taken a wave yet.

I jumped off the Jet Ski and sunk into the warm blue water. "They're coming in nicely. It'll be easy to paddle in." I grabbed my board off the trailer. "You coming?" I asked Esme.

"I'll paddle out with you," she said, rolling off the Jet Ski. "But I'm not going to ride those." She grabbed her board off the trailer.

"I'll wait here," Delgado said. "In case anyone gets in trouble." As we paddled away, Delgado shot over to one of the other Jet Skis and started talking with the driver.

"Do you think Kevin will be here?" Esme asked.

I looked at the waves and all the surfers lined up to fly down these monsters. "If he's on this island, or anywhere nearby, he'll be here," I said. A massive twenty-foot wave split from the main break, which can happen when the wind shifts or a wave comes in too quickly. The wave was headed right toward us.

"Luca!" Esme yelled. "What do we do?"

I held on to my board and was dragged up the front of the wave. At the last moment, I pushed down hard on the nose, hoping I would shoot through to the other side.

chapter twelve

As soon as I made it through the wave, I looked for Esme. She shot up over the crest of the wave and barreled down the backside. She rode her board like a boogie board and came up beside me.

"Where did that come from?" she said. She sounded rattled but excited.

"I have no idea," I said and laughed. It was exhilarating to be out here.

"Let's get out to where the rest of

the surfers are and see if Kevin's there," she said, paddling away from me.

I recognized a few of the surfers from the day before, but there were dozens I didn't know. People had swept in from around the world to challenge these waves. I overheard someone complain about the size. They had been expecting something bigger.

"Another hour, brah. Chill for another hour or two. These beasts are building," one guy said.

The waves were breaking in a half circle. They started in front of us and wrapped around to where the other break had been the day before. Now the break was just one giant one. The midsection was higher where the reef was. This drove the cresting wave directly into the black rocks, which, with the height and force of these waves, looked minuscule.

"You going in?" Esme asked.

"Sure," I said. "When it's my turn."

A couple of the other surfers turned to look at us. One of them had a devious smile.

"No turns here, brah. You want a wave today, you've got to take it," he said.

The guy beside him shoved him. "Don't listen to Jake," he said. "Dude just flew in from LA. Rude-surfer central. You want to take a wave, go for it, man. We're all just kind of figuring out the lay of the land."

"Thanks," I said. Another set was rolling in. It looked like the waves would be much the same size.

"Get on that," someone yelled.

I paddled into where the wave would crest.

As the wave approached, I paddled hard and stood just in time. I teetered on the crest and shot down the front. It was amazing. I cut to the right and rode the face of the wave before steering slightly up and then back down again. As the wave began to break, I had a moment in the barrel, then stormed forward and shot up the front of the wave, diving off my board and landing outside of where the next wave was cresting. I got back on my board, did a duck dive through the next wave and came out the other side to where the Jet Skis were bobbing.

"Very nice!" Delgado yelled. "Go get another one!"

I paddled back out to the lineup, and the mouthy guy from LA who had been a creep gave me a high five. "Nice ride," he said. "How is it?"

"Clean," I said. "Not messy at all. Like riding on a piece of glass."

What looked like the final wave of the set was rolling in. Jake, the guy from LA, started paddling out in front of the wave before it broke. He managed to stand up, but as he dropped in, he leaned too far forward and went headfirst into the wave.

"Ohhhh!" his friend yelled. "He just got owned out there, brah." He looked over at me. "Did you see that?"

"Yeah," I said. We waited for him to pop up. His board surfaced, but the guy was nowhere to be seen.

"Where is he?" his friend asked. He looked at me again. "Is it reef there or what?"

"Sand," I said. "For a long way."

Surfers die in these kinds of conditions all the time. They get swept under, dragged down and beaten against the floor of the ocean. But Jake popped up, coughing and sputtering.

"Brah," his friend yelled. "You all right?"

Jake looked at me. "Yeah." He grabbed his board and swam toward us. "Like glass out here, isn't that what you said?"

Another set came crashing in. It was unexpected, and the waves were much larger. The twenty-foot waves from before were now getting close to being forty-foot rollers.

Surfers paddled over to their Jet Skis and grabbed hold of the attached ropes. The Jet Skis' engines fired up and the waves crashed. Everything became intense. The waves loomed larger and spread out farther. With the roar of the Jet Skis and the pungent stench of fuel surrounding us, it seemed like we were in a different place.

"Here they come!" someone yelled.

"These are huge," Esme said as we paddled away from the edge of a wave.

It took a lot of effort to stay in the middle of this size of wave. It was best to keep to the side, where you could play spectator.

"They're building," I said. The next wave was over forty feet. It's possible to paddle into a wave that size, but easier to get towed.

"Hey," Jake yelled over to me.

"Yeah?" I said.

"You paddling in or towing?"

I looked at the wave, and no one else was paddling in. One bit of surfer etiquette rarely got forgotten in big waves: you don't tow into a big wave if other people are paddling in. It's too dangerous.

"I'm not paddling in," I yelled back as a wave crashed behind me.

"Go, go, go!" Jake said to his Jet Ski driver, and they headed toward the next rolling wave.

More surfers and Jet Skis were approaching. There were more people in the water than I had thought.

"There he is," Esme yelled.

"Who?"

"Kevin."

I looked to where she was pointing and sure enough, it was Kevin. He was being towed toward the backside of the wave. He was glowing.

"He's being towed by Jose," I said.

"What the hell is going on?" Esme asked.

"I don't know. But we'd better find out." I wasn't going to let either of them get away this time. "Let's wait here. They'll come around again," I said.

But Kevin turned and saw us. His face stiffened, and he looked away. I knew he would catch the next wave and disappear again. I wasn't going to let that happen.

"Damn," I said. "He saw us." I turned around to find Delgado a short distance away. "Delgado," I yelled. "Tow me in!"

Delgado glanced at the big waves and then back at me. "No way," he said. "These are monsters."

"I have to catch one of these waves," I said as we paddled up to his Jet Ski. Delgado turned the motor off. Kevin and Jose were doing slow circles at the edge of the wave, waiting for the right moment to drop in. We didn't have much time.

"Our friend is here," I said. "Tow me out so I can talk to him."

Delgado looked to where I was pointing. He shook his head and crossed his arms. "These waves are too big, and you, my friend, are too small."

We watched Jose tow Kevin into the wave. Kevin released the rope, dropped down the face of the wave and cut toward the rocks. There was only one way to catch up to him.

I had to surf.

chapter thirteen

"You have to tow me in, Delgado," I said.

He shook his head. "No, man, these are too big. I don't want to be the one who drags you to your death."

"I can surf these," I yelled.

"Remember, I was the one who patched you up yesterday? And those were tiny waves."

I glanced over at where I had last seen Kevin. He must have missed the wave, because he was still waiting his turn.

"It had nothing to do with the waves," I said, "and everything to do with someone cutting me off."

"Luca, Esme." I looked up to find Alana riding up on a Jet Ski.

"Alana," I said, turning away from Delgado. "Do you have a tow rope?"

She pulled a length of rope out of the seat compartment. "Sure do. I came out to see these waves. They're huge."

I paddled over. "Have you ever towed anyone into a wave?"

"A couple of times. I've towed a lot of wakeboards though."

"Perfect," I said. "Tow me into that, please."

"Really?" she said.

"They are too big, man!" Delgado said.

I was worried he was going to suddenly move his Jet Ski in front of us.

"Our friend is out there. He's about to take a wave. I have to talk to him," I said.

"And what if he catches the wave first?" Delgado asked.

I looked up to see Kevin barreling toward the top of the wave. "Then I will too," I said, grabbing the rope. "Go!"

We shot past three other Jet Skis. I wanted to grab the same wave as Kevin, but we got there too late. He was already shooting across the top, waiting to let go of the rope and drop in. Alana looked back at me.

"The next one," I yelled. "Take the next one."

The waves were fairly close together. They were also relentless. The sets kept coming with only the briefest of breaks between them. Alana shouted at other surfers, apologizing for cutting in line. And suddenly I was cruising across the top of a fifty-foot rolling, heaving mass of water that seemed to suck up everything in front of it. Alana looked over her shoulder. I gave her a thumbs-up, and when she cut to the back of the wave, I let go.

It was like falling off the side of a building. The board skipped beneath me.

I flew off bumps in the wave, taking air and landing. I was glad I had a board with footholds. My instinct was to cut to the right. But I knew Kevin had gone the other way. There was no telling how close I was to the rocks or the reef surrounding them. The wave was collapsing on itself as I shot forward. I carved to the left, and looked for a spot to cut out of the wake.

I pushed farther along the face and ducked as the wave collapsed and shot me out the end of the barrel across the shallow reef. The big black rocks were only fifteen or twenty feet away. I cut as hard as I could and weaved over the reef into deeper water.

I couldn't see Kevin anywhere. Behind me, surfers bobbed on the waves and watched the monsters rolling in. It was definitely calmer on this side of the reef. I scanned the beach, straining to see if Kevin was there or the Jet Ski Jose had been driving. But both Kevin and Jose had disappeared.

I heard the whine of Jet Skis coming to life, and watched as, in the distance, another giant wave rolled in. The surfers on this side of the reef paddled over to their Jet Skis. Moments later they were being towed out toward the break.

I tried to find Kevin in the crowd, but the next big wave was coming. I had to get off the reef quickly.

I paddled into the oncoming wave. I knew I would be knocked back when it came in, but I needed to put some distance between myself and the rocks, or I'd be crushed against them.

The first wave came in, and I caught only the foamy remains of it. But the next one was pushing in closer to shore, breaking later. These waves weren't breaking in the same spot. They collapsed eventually, but I couldn't tell where it would be. The second wave was strong and would break well past where the first one had. I was going to be right in the middle of the break.

I paddled hard. There was no way I would make it up the wall of water, but what choice did I have? I couldn't get to shore. And I couldn't hop on the wave and ride it either. I was going to be smashed into the rocks.

I spotted a couple of surfers catching the wave, cutting long lines down its face. I paddled harder, pulling myself through the water.

"Luca!" I looked up to find Alana on her Jet Ski. She threw a rope at me. "Hurry, before we get destroyed out here."

I grabbed the rope, jumped up and jammed my feet into the straps on my surfboard. "Go!" I yelled.

Alana gunned the engine and shot off.

Right into the approaching wave.

chapter fourteen

Alana leaned as far forward as she could and steered the Jet Ski up the front of the wave. I held on tight as the water foamed and curled beneath me. When Alana disappeared over the lip of the wave, I crouched but was slung into the air. I landed on the back side of the wave, wobbling side to side.

Alana slowed down and looked over her shoulder at me. "We have to cut across the wave," she yelled, pointing to the far side, where the other Jet Skis and surfers were bobbing about. I spun in a slow circle, trying to keep some momentum so I wouldn't sink. "Hold on," she said and turned the Jet Ski around.

Suddenly we were flying through the valley between waves, the next giant wall of water already bearing down on us. The water was choppy. I struggled to hold on. If I bailed, I was done for. The coming wave would suck me in and spit me out the back after it had raked me across the reef. No one would be pulling me out of the waves here. There might not be a lot of me left to even pull out.

A forty-foot wave closed in on us. Alana veered away from it. I scanned the top of the wave, where some surfers were launching from. I was certain I spotted Kevin.

"Alana!" I yelled.

She glanced back. I pointed at the top of the wave.

"The next one, you adrenaline junkie!" she screamed.

The wave was breaking right to left, and luckily we were on the outside when it collapsed. Alana slowed down again.

I let go of the rope and drifted up beside her. "I think Kevin got on that wave."

We watched surfers forced toward the reef by the collapsing wave. "That one broke the wrong way," Alana said. "They'll be driven into the reef and those rocks."

"Not if they cut soon enough. Then they'll end up on the other side."

"What do you want to do?"

"I need to take the next wave." I grabbed the rope. "Can you tow me in?"

"You're crazy, Luca. I can't tow you in there. Those waves are pushing sixty feet."

I was filled with adrenaline. I had never surfed waves this big before. There was no way to work up to these giants. You just had to do it.

"He'll disappear again," I said. I shook the rope. "Please." She looked at me, then back at the wave. "Come on, Alana." I clung to the side of the Jet Ski, my face turned toward her.

She leaned over and kissed me on the mouth.

"That's just in case I never get another chance," she said. "Hold on." She gunned the Jet Ski, and we shot toward the next wave.

To get on a big wave you have to cut along the side of the break and steer into it at just the right spot. If we went in too late, the wave would break and both of us would drop sixty feet onto the exposed reef. Big waves pull everything into them, including fish, sharks, logs, bottles and cans. Once I even saw a mannequin rolling in the face of a wave.

Alana approached the wave slowly. She gunned forward and then let off a bit as we drew toward it. "Here we go," she yelled.

The mass of water rolled up beside us. As we approached the lip, another Jet Ski flew past. I was turning into the wave, preparing for the dizzying drop, when I looked over and saw Kevin smiling.

"Kevin," I yelled.

His smile faded. "Luca, what are you doing here?" he yelled.

"Let go!" Alana yelled. The wave was cresting. She needed to take off before she went over with it. I let go after Kevin did, and the two of us dropped.

The wave was messier than the first one I had taken. Kevin immediately cut to the right. I was more interested in outrunning it. The wave was breaking from right to left again, so I followed Kevin toward the rocks. Kevin had cut back up the front of the wave. He was carving back and forth as though he was on a six- or seven-foot wave. I kept going straight down, thinking only of getting to shore as quickly as possible. Kevin would have to come in. He had seen me, and he knew I'd seen him. If he didn't come in, then I had no idea who he was anymore.

I glanced over my shoulder at Kevin. He was carving, rushing ahead of the barrel. I focused on the shore, feeling the press of the massive wave behind me. The wave slowed, and I glanced back.

Kevin was gone.

chapter fifteen

I carved out of the wave and lay down on my board. My heart was thumping. But I didn't have long to rest. The next wave was coming in, and it looked angry.

I couldn't see Kevin anywhere, just white foaming water where the wave had crashed. I looked toward the shallow reef and spotted a surfboard, just the tip, bobbing in the foam. But I didn't see Kevin. I started to swim back out. Where was Jose on his Jet Ski? He was supposed to make sure Kevin came up on the other side.

I heard the whine of an engine, and Alana was beside me, standing tall on her Jet Ski. "Where's your friend?" she yelled.

"I don't know. He didn't come out. There's a bit of his board over there." The next wave crashed down. I clung to the side of the Jet Ski until the surge passed. I looked at the rocks once the water had receded. Something moved. I paddled out to get a better look. It was Kevin, clinging to the side of a rock.

"He's over there!" I yelled.

"There's another wave coming in. He's going to get battered," said Alana.

"We have to go get him," I said, releasing my board and pulling myself up on the Jet Ski.

"There'll be no room for him if we both go," Alana said. She rolled off the Jet Ski into the water. "You go get him." She grabbed hold of my board, pulled herself onto it and started paddling to shore.

I slid forward, clamped the gas and shot off. The reef was almost entirely exposed. The bottom of the Jet Ski hit the coral briefly and whined as the jets sucked air. The next wave was pulling hard. I could feel the force of it under the Jet Ski as I drew closer to the rocks. Kevin tried to climb on top of the rock to avoid being crashed by the incoming wave. I turned sharply and cut toward the rocks.

"Kevin!" I yelled. I was twenty feet from the rock. The wave was beginning to break. "Get ready to jump!"

The Jet Ski smashed into the reef again, bounced into the air and landed in deeper water. It struck another bit of the reef and screamed to a halt.

Kevin looked at the wave. "Get out of here, Luca! You're not going to make it."

I rocked back and forth, fighting with the Jet Ski. It was stuck on a cleft in the reef. I needed to tilt it off. I didn't look at the incoming wave. There was nothing I could do but get the Jet Ski off the reef and move out of the way.

"Get ready to jump!" I yelled again.

I stepped on the reef and felt the slice of a sharp edge on my ankle. Water trickled under the ski. Soon the wave would smash on top of us, plowing Kevin and me into the rocks. There was no way we would survive. I had to get the Jet Ski off the reef.

I jammed my foot painfully onto the coral. The Jet Ski didn't move. I got off, gunned the gas and pushed as hard as I could. Somehow the ski shifted off the reef into deeper water. I flung myself back on and leaned forward. I was five feet away from the rock. "Jump, Kevin. Jump!"

Kevin dropped down and landed on the back of the Jet Ski. The impact of his weight on the rear of the Jet Ski thrust us forward. We cleared the rocks just as the wave swept in. I turned toward shore, and we cruised in on the wave's power.

I let the Jet Ski glide in to shore. When we reached shallow water, Kevin jumped off and sprinted up the shoreline. I pulled the key from the ignition and took off after him. Kevin and I had played this game before. Tag, touch football, soccer, it didn't matter—I was faster than him. Even with torn-up feet, I caught up with him and knocked him to the sand. He rolled over and pushed me off.

I pinned his arms down with my knees and leaned back on his stomach. "What the hell are you doing?" I yelled at him.

"Get off. He can't see you with me."

"Who? What are you talking about?"

Kevin struggled to get free. "Man, I never should have ridden that wave. I knew you'd be out there."

"Kevin, what are you talking about? What's wrong with you?"

He was looking out to where the other Jet Skis bobbed in the water. "Follow me into the jungle," he said, trying to shift me off him again.

"What? No way."

"Please, Luca, you don't understand. It's...My parents are alive. I am so close to..."

"What?" I shifted off him slightly.

Blood dribbled down his forehead. He was breathing in quick gulps. His arms were all marked up from where he had smashed against the rock.

"He has my parents, Luca. They're alive."

chapter sixteen

I rolled off him into the sand as Alana walked up with my board under her arm.

"You survived?" she said.

"Just," I said.

"And this must be the mythical Kevin."

Kevin looked at his arms and legs. Blood mixed with the salt water on his skin.

"What are you talking about, Kevin? Your parents are alive?" I said.

He looked out at the surfers and Jet Skis again. "Just come into the jungle, Luca.

We'll go behind those palms so he can't see me."

"Who, Kevin? Who can't see you?" I asked.

"Delgado."

I followed Kevin into the jungle and sat on a log. Alana stayed on the beach with the Jet Ski and my board.

"What is this all about?" I asked.

Kevin peered around a palm. The beach was still empty. A few surfers were being pulled in, either beaten and worn from riding the waves or having decided they weren't good enough to be out there in the first place.

"Where is he?" Kevin asked.

"Who?"

"Delgado. You were with him, right?"

"He's still out there, as far as I know. He wouldn't tow me into the wave."

"And where's Esme?"

"With him, I guess. Why?" I asked.

Kevin stared at me. "He...he has my parents. They came down here to get away from that stupid investigation. They didn't die in the plane crash. Are you sure Esme didn't come in?"

"Who told you they're still alive?" I asked.

"Delgado. But it makes sense. My dad is a good pilot. He would have known how to crash land a plane in bad weather."

"Wait," I said. "Back up. Delgado contacted you? When?"

"About six months ago. He called and told me my parents had survived and were in hiding. He was protecting them. He said they couldn't contact me because they thought I was being watched and my phone and email monitored."

"But no one noticed he called you?"

"I don't know, Luca. Delgado was very cryptic. I came down here so I could talk to him."

"Why didn't you contact the police?"

"If I had talked to anyone in the US and they found out my parents were alive, they would have arrested them."

It all seemed so crazy. "So, Delgado contacted you and...what? What does he want from you?"

"He wants to finish my parents' hotel on the other side of the island."

"We saw it," I said. "I didn't know your dad had invested in a place here."

"The plan is for Delgado to run it. This area is becoming a destination spot. And with the waves here, the hotel will be filled with surfers year-round. The hotel wasn't part of my dad's business. It was something he was doing on the side. My parents wanted to retire down here. But Delgado said they had to get away from the investigation, so they staged the plane crash. But after the crash, construction had to stop."

"What exactly was the investigation about?"

"My dad was being investigated for some kind of fraud. I guess he figured eventually someone would find out about the hotel and it would be taken away from him, like everything else was. So he put it in Delgado's name. Not that my dad is guilty. The whole investigation is bogus anyway."

"I figured it was. Your dad is a good person."

"Exactly. The government thinks my dad has been defrauding a group of investors. But he didn't know anything about it. Before they came down to Panama, he caught one of his managers doing something illegal. But it was going to be impossible to prove my dad didn't know what had been happening. So he and my mom came down here for a while. Until things calmed down."

I didn't understand the business world Mr. Taylor moved in. He was a great surfer and a good guy. He wouldn't have been involved in something underhanded. "Why didn't you come here with them?" I asked.

"I was supposed to meet up with them later, after graduation."

"I don't get it. If your parents are here, what does Delgado need you for?"

"Because of my parents' life insurance." Kevin looked away. The waves were coming in heavy, heaving swells. I watched as a surfer was tossed off his board and disappeared into the angry, frothing mess of a wave.

"What about the life insurance?" I asked.

"Who's the blond you're with?" Kevin asked.

"Alana. We just met the other day."

Kevin winked at me. "She's hot."

"Yeah, and back to you, Kevin. What about your parents' life insurance?"

"I've been giving it all to Delgado to help finish the hotel. But I can only take out a certain amount every month. So it may be a couple of weeks before we can get the construction going again. And then I'll get to see my parents."

"Kevin, how do you even know that...?"

He stared at me. "That my parents are alive?"

"Yeah."

"I just know, Luca. I just know. Delgado says it's better if I don't see them. There was too much heat from the investigation. When the construction is done and the investigators have figured out what actually happened with my dad's business, then we can be together again."

"So you are certain...?"

"Luca," Kevin said. He leaned against the tree and stared at the ground. His hair had grown out and dangled in front of his face. "What else am I supposed to believe?" He spun around and looked back out at the break.

Alana came up from the beach and approached the log. "Are you two okay?"

"Yeah, but could you go out and see if Esme and Delgado are still at the break?" I asked.

"Sure." She tilted her head to one side. "Are you coming with me?"

"No, I need to stay here," I said, handing her the key.

Kevin looked at me again. "I'm not going anywhere. You caught me."

Alana took off toward the water. A moment later she was bouncing out toward the break on her Jet Ski.

"It all makes sense," Kevin said. "You have to admit it does."

"I guess," I said, but I was skeptical. I knew Kevin's dad, and he never would have run from a fight. Not even one with federal investigators. He loved LA. I couldn't see him chucking everything, including his only son, to run away from an investigation. "Do you have any proof they're alive, Kevin? Anything at all?"

He banged his chest. "I know it, Luca. They're here."

Alana disappeared behind the waves. I felt a tinge of panic for her. The waves were big, and it wasn't easy to steer a Jet Ski through them.

"Why did you run away from us?" I asked.

"Delgado said not to speak to anyone for a while. He said anyone might have been sent to investigate me and the plane crash. This is a big money thing."

"I don't doubt it." I spotted Alana coming back in from the other break. She must have gone out one side, then cut across and searched the other line as well. She pulled the Jet Ski up to the beach.

"You can come out of there," she called from the shore. "They're gone."

"What?" Kevin said. "Crap. He must have seen us together. Now...Where's Jose?

I need to talk to him." Kevin came around the tree and down onto the beach. He tried to grab the Jet Ski key from Alana.

"He's not out there either," Alana said, pulling the key to her stomach.

"Where did he go?" Kevin asked.

Alana stepped away from him. "I don't know. But all three of them are gone."

Kevin looked at me, his face blank and beaten. Blood was smeared across his forehead. "Where did they go, Luca?" he said. "What's happened?"

"I think they've got Esme," I said.

He looked up and down the beach. "Maybe they came in to shore and we didn't see them. Let's go to Delgado's house and see if they're there."

chapter seventeen

We moved through the jungle to the edge of the beach in front of Delgado's hut. Delgado and Jose's Jet Skis weren't there, but two boats were.

"Can you see anyone?" Kevin asked.

There wasn't any movement around Delgado's. "No," I said. "Let's go to my hut. We can see inside Delgado's from there." We continued along the edge of the jungle and darted inside my hut.

"There's no one in Delagado's," Alana said.

Kevin looked at me. "Luca, where did they take her?"

I didn't want to say anything, but it was hard not to point out the obvious. "I have a feeling Delgado isn't telling you the whole truth," I said.

"What do you mean?"

"Isn't it clear? He needs your inheritance to finish the hotel for himself, to run on his own."

"No, he's protecting my parents. He's hiding them from the investigators and helping them finish the hotel. He's keeping them safe, that's all."

"So why would he take Esme?"

Kevin sat down on the bed and put his head in his hands. "I don't know. Maybe he thinks Esme is here to turn in my parents." He looked up at us. "We have to wait. He'll be back. He wants to run the hotel with my parents. It means everything to him."

"So much that he has taken your parents and Esme hostage?" I said.

Kevin shook his head and scowled. "Not hostage," he said. "They're hiding in case someone comes down here to investigate. He's protecting them, covering for them."

"It sounds dodgy," I said, but he didn't seem to hear me. "Have you even seen any paperwork for the hotel? Are you sure Delgado's name is on it?"

"They're at the hotel!" he said. "That's where Delgado would take Esme. He's probably just making sure she isn't a federal investigator or something." Kevin was up and out the door without another word.

"This is crazy," Alana said.

"Welcome to my life," I said as we ran after him.

The hotel was empty. Kevin ran from room to room calling out Esme's name. He had been camping out in the hotel.

"What now, Kevin?" I said.

"We wait until Jose and Delgado bring Esme here. That's what will happen," said Kevin. "They aren't criminals. They wouldn't do anything to her."

"Are you sure?" I asked.

"Yes, Delgado's not...he's not like that."

"Well," Alana said, "I'm hungry. I'm going to get us some food. You know, just in case they don't get here for a while."

She disappeared down the beach toward the village. Kevin and I sat and watched the waves roll in, one after another, in that slow, mesmerizing way they do. It was easy to see why someone would build a hotel here.

"You've been living here?" I asked.

"Yeah. In one of the more finished rooms. Jose brings me water and stuff."

"Why?"

"Why does he bring me water?"

"No, why are you living here? Why not stay at Delgado's?"

"I wanted to be here in case someone came to look at the hotel. Like a federal investigator or whatever. Then we'd know if anyone was onto it. But no one has shown up yet."

"I still don't get why you can't just be with your parents if they're hiding out."

"We have to make sure no one is watching me."

I looked around at the swaying palm trees and barren beach. If anyone was watching Kevin, they were doing so with an incredible amount of stealth.

Alana returned with a lobster, mahimahi and fresh fruit. We started a fire and cooked everything together in a pot. The sweetness of the fruit blended with the lobster meat and fish. We ate quickly, starving after the energy we'd used on the waves.

"We'll wait for Jose," Kevin said every few minutes. "You'll see, everything will be fine." I couldn't take it anymore. I had to say something. "Jose. The same Jose who cut me off in a wave and drove me onto the reef yesterday? He almost killed me. Plus, I trashed my board. That's when I saw you on the beach."

"Jose had nothing to do with it," Kevin said. "He helped drag you to shore."

"So where was he when I was rammed into the reef?"

"He was surfing. He was..." Kevin looked up at the perfectly blue sky. "No, he was on the other side of the break."

"No, he dropped in, cut me off and then shot to the other side. Who got to me first?"

"I did," Kevin said. "I was on the beach. I was hoping you would call it a day so I could go back out."

"And you didn't notice who blasted me into the reef?"

"No, I must have been in the jungle. Answering the call of nature."

"Well, it was Jose who drove me into those rocks. I almost died out there," I said.

"No. Jose wouldn't do that," Kevin said, shaking his head.

"Kevin, who are you going to believe? We've known each another all our lives." I ate a bit of lobster and a square of mango and tried to contain my anger.

"It must have been a mistake," said Kevin. He nodded, agreeing with himself. "It had to be." He looked out at the dock.

The empty lanterns swung in the breeze. "He'll be here, and he'll have Esme with him. You'll see. Everything is going to be good."

Alana was silent. Eventually she got up and sat at the end of the dock. I followed her out.

"He really believes his parents are here, doesn't he?" she said.

"Wouldn't you?"

"I would want to. Sure. But..." She kicked her feet in the water. "What do you think?"

"I don't know," I said. "I guess it's possible."

"Yeah, kind of, in that 'anything is possible' way."

"Maybe."

"Shouldn't we be out there looking for Esme?"

I thought about this for a minute. "Even if this whole parents being hidden thing is bogus, I don't see Delgado as some kind of crazy killer or anything. I'm sure if he has Esme, she's fine."

"Sure?" Alana asked.

"As sure as I can be."

We waited until the afternoon sun descended, and then we walked back up to the hotel.

"I guess they aren't coming," Kevin said. "Okay, you're right, Luca."

I put a hand on his shoulder. "I don't know. Maybe your parents are alive. Delgado might not be lying. But it doesn't look good. We've waited long enough. We have to do something. We have to find Esme and make sure she is all right. Can you think of anywhere else Delgado and Jose might have taken her? Did he ever tell you where your parents were hiding?"

"No. He said it wasn't safe for me to know. Just in case agents came to talk to me," Kevin said.

"But do you have any idea? Any idea at all?" I asked.

Kevin stared at the water. "Yeah, maybe."

"Where?" Alana asked.

"Another island. It's over on the other side. Maybe twenty minutes by boat," Kevin said.

"What's so special about this particular island?" I asked.

"I was at Delgado's once, and he had a map up on his computer screen. It was zeroed in on that island. That's all I know."

Alana looked at me. "It's all we have to go on," she said.

"So," I said, "we call the Panamanian police and..."

"No," Kevin said, "we can't call the police. They're all friends with Delgado. Haven't you noticed them hanging out on the beach? They protect Delgado for some reason."

"Okay, then we go out to the island," I said. "Alana, do you still have the Jet Ski?"

Alana nodded. "I rented it for three days."

"We'll need a trailer on it," I said.

"Yeah, there is a trailer for it," she said.

I patted Kevin on the back. "Come on, bro. Let's go find Esme. And clear all this up."

Kevin nodded. I could tell he didn't want to go. It was easier for him to believe his parents were on another island, sipping mango juice and soaking up the sun, than it was to discover Delgado was lying.

chapter eighteen

We waited until it was dark. It would be dangerous, but we didn't want to tip off Delgado. Before we left, we checked Delgado's house again. No one was around. We hooked the trailer to Alana's Jet Ski and pushed it into the water. I loaded our boards onto the trailer and got on behind Alana. Kevin lay on top of the boards.

We moved along the shoreline until we had passed the reef. Alana cut straight out into deeper waters. The waves had calmed down, and we could hear people partying at the Purple Parrot.

Once we were out past the reef, the only sounds were of the Jet Ski pushing through the waves. Luckily, it was loud enough that talking was virtually impossible. I glanced back at Kevin a couple of times. It took about half an hour to reach the island. It was impossible to bring the Jet Ski in close to the rocky shoreline. If Delgado and Jose were here, they must have landed on a different beach.

Alana cut the engine, and we drifted across the surface. "I can't get any closer," she said. "You'll have to paddle in."

"Look," Kevin said, pointing to the shore. "There's a light."

"Where?" I asked.

"To the right."

I squinted at where he was pointing and thought I could make out a tiny glow in the jungle. "Okay," I said. "Let's go."

Alana grabbed my arm and kissed me. "I'll wait out here."

"That would be great," I said.

"For you, anything." She gave me a crooked smile as I rolled off the Jet Ski and into the water.

Kevin already had the boards off the trailer. "Let's try to go in on the side here," he said, pointing. "Try to end up over there." He pointed at a spot at the far edge of the beach. "We'll have to dump our boards and keep low. They might be watching for us."

"Kevin, you know everything Delgado told you might not be true?"

"I'm not ready to accept that," Kevin said. "But I still think it's best if no one sees us come ashore."

"Who is Jose anyway? I mean, what's his role in all of this?"

"I don't know," Kevin said. "He works with Delgado around the hotel. That's all I know." He looked over his shoulder at the approaching waves. "Paddle when the waves are high, okay? We should be able to make it over the reef that way."

The first wave came in, and we paddled hard, staying on top as long as possible until it passed. In the lull between waves, we were stuck on the top of the reef. I kept my arms and legs out of the water, not wanting to get cut any more than I already was. I wasn't all that concerned with what the reef would do to the bottom of Delgado's board.

It took awhile, but eventually we made it in to the shore. I looked back out where we'd left Alana and couldn't see her. It was a dark night. The bit of moonlight on the water illuminated fish scooting around the reef. I picked my board up and kept low. The sand had already cooled after the hot day. I carried my board toward the rocks Kevin had pointed out. He was kneeling behind one of the larger rocks, his surfboard on the ground beside him. I dropped my board next to his and crouched down.

"I think I saw something move over there," Kevin said.

"When?" I whispered.

"Just as you walked up."

We waited, staring into the darkness. As my eyes adjusted to the night landscape, I too thought I could see something at the edge of the jungle. Something, or someone, moving around.

"Right there?" I whispered.

Kevin tapped my arm. A sign to be quiet. I tried not to move. The cool air chilled my damp skin. The moon had broken through the clouds, although it was only a crescent.

"What should we do?" I said.

Kevin put his hand on my arm again. There was a flash of light in the jungle where I thought I had seen something move. And suddenly I recognized Jose's profile as he lit a cigarette.

"We're going to have to take him down," Kevin said.

"But what if you're right?" I said. "What if Delgado's protecting your parents rather than holding them hostage?"

"Then I'll have to apologize to him," he said and ran across the beach.

chapter nineteen

Kevin moved silently. I followed him, but for the first time, I wasn't able to catch up. He launched himself at Jose.

"Kevin!" I said.

By the time I reached them, Kevin was sitting on Jose's chest, holding his arms down. "Where are they?" he said.

Jose shook sand off his face. "What? What are you doing, man?" he said.

"You speak English!" I said.

"Of course I do, brah. I'm from LA."

"Where are they?" Kevin said, shaking Jose.

"Get off, man."

"Where are they?" Kevin said again.

"Who?" Jose looked at me. "Who is he looking for?"

"Esme and his parents," I said.

Jose seemed unable to look directly at Kevin. "I don't know about that, man."

"What do you mean?" Kevin asked.

"I...man, I don't know..."

"Is there a house or something here?" I asked.

"Yeah. Back there."

Kevin grabbed Jose's throat. "Who's inside?"

"Delgado and that girl," Jose squeaked.

Kevin squeezed Jose's face in his hands. "That girl is my girlfriend. And you better not have laid a finger on her. Who else is in there?"

"No one," Jose said.

"Are you sure?" I asked.

"It's a two-room hut, brah. Kinda hard to hide." Kevin raised his fist above his head.

Jose winced and screwed his eyes shut. "Come on, man. You don't want to hit me."

"Kevin," I said.

Kevin looked at me and then back at Jose. "You stay out here, or I swear I will pound you into the ground."

"Whatever," Jose said.

"Not whatever, Jose." Kevin stood, and Jose rolled out from beneath him.

"Okay, okay, man. I'll stay right here. I'm through with all of this anyway. It's gotten too weird." Jose picked his cigarette up off the sand and pulled his lighter out. Then he leaned back and started smoking as though nothing had happened.

"Come on," Kevin said to me and took off through the jungle.

Crabs scattered as we ran through the thick growth. A lantern inside the house flickered.

"No electricity out here," Kevin whispered. We crept to the side of the house. It was a solid wood structure with a window or two on each side. There was a porch with a lantern dangling from a hook and, inside, another three or four lanterns illuminated a living room. "Let's check around the back."

At the rear of the house was a door with no steps leading from it. The house wasn't on stilts. It looked like a set of stairs had never been built to the door. In fact, as we got closer, the whole house looked half finished. The door was open, and the smell of boiled fish wafted out. Kevin crept to the bottom of the doorway and peered in.

He waved me over.

"Do you like hot sauce?" we heard Delgado say. "Okay, Miss Esme, I will continue to talk to myself. I will not put hot sauce in the stew and, instead, will place it on the table so everyone can make up his or her own mind." I peered in the door and saw a kitchen. Delgado was only five feet away, with his back to us, and a giant pot steaming before him. "Now, I'm going to untie you so you can eat. Do you promise to be good?"

Again there was no response. I pictured Esme tied up in the other room, refusing to speak.

Delgado heaped rice onto a plate, stirred the pot again and dumped a spoonful of fish stew on top. He filled a second plate, gathered up some cutlery and picked up both plates. "Promise or not, Miss Esme, you aren't going anywhere," he said and disappeared from the kitchen. "Not yet. Not until I figure out what to do next anyway."

"Come on," Kevin said, putting his palms on the edge of the doorway. He climbed up into the kitchen and quickly moved to the opposite wall.

"You can go to hell," I heard Esme yell, and a plate smashed.

Atta girl, I thought. I was about to pull myself up when Jose came out of the trees and tackled me to the ground.

"Delgado, they're here!" Jose yelled.

I was face-first in the dirt. I struggled to get away. Jose had his hand on the back of my head, pushing my face into the sand. I stayed still for a moment, and his grip let up. I waited another moment.

"You just stay there," Jose said.

I couldn't see which way he was facing, but I felt him shift his body slightly to one side. It took all my strength, but I managed to kick Jose off and roll over at the same time.

"So you found us," Delgado said.

"Where are they?" Kevin demanded.

I brushed sand from my face and eyes. Jose was beside me. He didn't seem to know what to do. I pushed my hands into the sand and kicked him as hard as I could. He tumbled to the ground.

"Didn't we tell you to stay put?" I said, standing up. I stepped on his chest and launched myself through the doorway.

chapter twenty

"Put the knife down, Kevin," Delgado said as I entered the living room.

Kevin had a fishing knife, dripping with fish guts, gripped in one hand. "Where are they?" he said.

"Kevin," I said. But he wasn't listening. I heard rustling behind me and turned in time to grab Jose and dump him on the floor. Kevin didn't even turn around.

"Put the knife down, man," Jose said. He rolled into the corner and pulled his legs to his chest. "Come on, this has gone far enough. Just put the knife down."

I moved against the wall so I could keep an eye on Jose—though he didn't look like he was going anywhere.

"Kevin," Esme said. "What are you doing? Put the knife down."

Kevin took a step toward Delgado. "I'm only going to ask you once. Where are my parents?"

"Put the knife down, Kevin, or you'll never know." He snapped his fingers. "I can make them disappear like that."

Esme stood up and came around the end of the table. "Kevin, put the knife down." A piece of cloth that must have been used as a gag hung around her neck. A length of rope dangled from her wrist.

"Don't be stupid, man. Put the knife down," Jose said.

"Kevin," I said.

"Kevin," Esme said.

But he wasn't hearing us. He charged at Delgado, the knife raised. Delgado turned and put his hands up in front of his face. Kevin hit Delgado's throat with his forearm, dragged him to the ground and smacked his head. There were tears on his cheeks. His eyes were red and his lips quivered. Delgado held his hands in front of his face. "Where are they?" he shouted and smacked Delgado on the head again. "Where are they? Where are they?" Delgado turned to one side and coughed. "Just tell me where they are!"

I looked at Delgado, and I knew. I had known all along, even though I had hoped it wasn't true. I had believed as much as I could. But not as much as Kevin had. "They died, Kevin," I said. "Right, Delgado?"

Delgado nodded, and Kevin dropped the knife. Esme grabbed it and set it on the table behind her.

"Just like in the newspaper reports, right?" I said.

Delgado nodded. Kevin rose, and Delgado scurried backward. He pulled himself to a seated position against the wall beside Jose.

"Why?" Kevin said. "Why would you give me all this...hope?"

"What was I supposed to do? I had everything tied up in that hotel. Sure, my huts are all right, but I barely keep my head above water."

"Why didn't you ask for help?" I said. "Rather than put everyone through all of this?"

Delgado pushed himself up the wall and shook his head. "Who would believe me?"

"So you emotionally blackmailed Kevin?" I said. "With the one thing you knew he cared most about? You thought that was a better idea? How long was this going to go on for?"

"Until the hotel was finished."

"And then what?" Esme said.

"I...I hadn't thought that far ahead."

Kevin stood up and pulled Esme to him. He put his arm around her waist and walked toward the door. I grabbed the knife off the table and followed them.

"I'm...I'm sorry," Delgado called. "Your father believed in that hotel. He loved Bocas. He wanted to share the island's waves with other surfers. He wanted to live here with you..."

Kevin looked at Delgado. "And that isn't going to happen. Just stay away from us, Delgado."

"I'm sorry. I really am. But what choice did I have?"

"You could have been kind," I said, repeating what Delgado had said to us when we had arrived.

I grabbed the lantern from the front porch and walked to the water's edge. The beach was cool and quiet. Palms swayed in the breeze as the waves rolled in, gently pushing against the shore. I held the lantern up and waved it from side to side. Kevin and Esme found our boards. I heard the rumble of an engine, and the headlight on Alana's Jet Ski flashed on and off.

"Here you go," Esme said. She handed me my board.

"All four of us won't be able to go back on the one Jet Ski," I said. "How about you guys wait here. I'll go in with Alana and then come back out."

Esme looked at Kevin. He didn't seem to be with us. "You think we'll be safe?" she asked.

"Yeah," I said. "I'm sure you will." I handed the knife to Kevin. "I'll be back in an hour. Okay?"

"Okay," Esme said. She took Kevin's hand and led him down the beach. "Thanks, Luca."

I dropped my board into the surf. The water was still warm. The clouds had parted, and the moon shone brilliantly on the water. I looked down at the sting rays and scurrying fish and paddled out into the deeper water.

"Where is everyone?" Alana asked as she helped me slide my board onto the trailer.

"Just Kevin and Esme," I said.

"No parents?"

"No parents." I climbed on behind her and wrapped my arms around her waist. "Can I use the Jet Ski to come back for them?"

"Hmm," she said, turning and presenting her lips. "For a price." I kissed her and held her tightly. "Was Delgado there?"

"Yeah. And Jose. Apparently they worked together on this."

"It sounds like it's a mess."

"It is," I said.

She gunned the Jet Ski, and we skipped out away from the breakers. "Anyway, if they're both here, then there's no one to stop us from grabbing Delgado's boat and coming back. It would be safer than the Jet Ski."

I kissed the back of her head. "Thank you," I said.

"Hey," she said. "What did I say? Anything for you."

chapter twenty-one

"Pass me that hammer," Kevin said. It was three weeks later, and we were hammering nails into the hotel's walls to hang paintings. Every painting was of the ocean. The beauty and power of the ocean was present in every room.

"How many more of these do we have left to hang?" I asked.

"This is the last one," Kevin said.

"No, it isn't," Esme said. "There's still one left to hang in the manager's room."

Kevin hammered a nail into the wall and hung another painting. "That room is going to get its own special treatment," he said, winking at Esme.

"Oh, is it now?" she said.

"Oh, it is," Kevin said crossing the room and bringing Esme into his arms.

We had decided to stay at the hotel to help Kevin complete his parents' dream. My parents weren't big on the idea of my staying in Panama, especially after everything that had happened. But Esme's dad was coming down early next week to help us get the hotel up and running.

Kevin hired locals to finish the construction. Delgado had "sold" the hotel to Kevin for nothing. And Kevin, in turn, had decided not to report Delgado to the police. The hotel would be operational in another month, six weeks at the most. And the locals, now involved in the building and, eventually, running of the hotel, were supportive of it. Kevin also had plans to give part of the hotel's annual profits to the village.

"Let's take a break," Kevin said.

I straightened the painting and followed them out to the beach. We walked the length of the pier to the dock, where there were twenty big chairs with cushions and side tables and a giant canopy for shade.

"It's almost done," I said, settling into a chair with a sigh.

"Yeah," Kevin said. "Can you imagine this place with people in it? Like, packed?"

"With surfers?" Esme said. "I don't want to imagine." She leaned against the railing. "Maybe filled with families. You know, kids and everything."

"You wouldn't know what to do with kids," Kevin said, laughing. Esme gave him a quick punch on the shoulder.

"Kids? You teach them to surf," Alana shouted. She stepped onto the pier in a floppy T-shirt and white shorts.

"No way," I said. "You want to turn the next generation into a bunch of useless beach bums?"

Alana settled into the chair beside me. She had decided to stick around too.

Her original plan to take a year off after graduation and travel with her boyfriend had shifted dramatically. Now, she said, she was going to stay in one place with her real boyfriend.

Alana looked at me. "Those five guys—I totally forget their names—the five we hired the other day?"

"Don't ask me. You set it up," I said.

"Well, the five guys who are supposed to come and do the concrete deck are coming tomorrow," she said.

"That's what they said yesterday," Kevin said.

She shrugged. "Busy guys, I guess."

Kevin laughed. "It'll all get done in time," he said, leaning over the railing beside Esme.

"And then what?" Esme said.

"Then we open Fallbrook Resort." He turned to face us. "Man, that has a nice ring to it."

"Your mom would love it," Esme said.

"She would," Kevin said. "My dad too. He always wanted me to go into business with him. I thought it would be super boring and, you know, corporate."

"Corporate?" I asked. "What does that even mean?"

He laughed. "Business-guy like."

Staying in Panama wasn't the worst idea in the world. I had options, of course. I had done well at high school and could apply to colleges, if I wanted. But for now, there was something appealing about island life. It was slow and steady and pleasant. And we were doing something to contribute to the community.

"Shrimp bake tonight?" Alana said. She had taken on the role of cook.

"Sounds perfect," I said.

Kevin wrapped an arm around Esme and looked back out at the water. He raised his head suddenly, like a dog who had heard a whistle. "Smell that?" he said.

I sniffed at the hot, heavy air. "What?"

"That's the smell of waves coming in." He closed his eyes. "Yes. Listen."

We all closed our eyes. I could hear birds in the trees, music from the village, the clicking sway of the palms. But nothing else. Not right away.

Then I heard it.

Beneath everything was the gentle lull of the ocean. The sleek, beautiful sound of approaching waves.

"Oh yeah," I said.

"You hear it?" Kevin said.

"Yeah. I hear it," I said.

Alana grabbed my hand and squeezed it. "Me too. Ten-footers I'd say."

"At least," Esme said. "I'd say up to twelve."

"No way. Those are easily fifteen feet," I said. "Twenty maybe."

"Monsters," Kevin said.

I opened my eyes. He was grinning at me.

"Want to go surfing?" he asked.

I smiled. "I thought you'd never ask."

Acknowledgments

Thanks go out to the usual suspects: Megan, Luca and Alex for making everything better; Christi Howes for her ninja-like editing abilities; the Paterson clan, Rebecca Van Vlasselaer, and the people of Bocas del Toro for an amazing time in Panama; as well as Luca and Kevin for lending their names.

Jeff Ross grew up near Collingwood, Ontario, where he learned to ski, snowboard, skateboard and injure himself in fantastic and unique ways. *Dawn Patrol* is his third novel in the Orca Sports series—all of which feature sports that involve standing sideways on a board. Jeff teaches English and Scriptwriting for Television and Animation at Algonquin College in Ottawa, Ontario. He is humored on a daily basis by his wife and two sons. Visit www.jeffrossbooks.com for more information.

ALSO AVAILABLE BY
JEFF ROSS

978-1-55469-392-4 pb
978-1-55469-393-1 pdf
978-1-4598-0033-5 epub

ALEX'S GOAL IN LIFE IS SIMPLE—
to snowboard all day, every day. His ultimate dream is to be part of the Backcountry Patrol, an elite group of snowboarders who patrol the ungroomed slopes of British Columbia. But first, he and three other young hopefuls (Dave, Bryce and Hope) must endure a series of tests that takes them to remote and dangerous terrain, where they must confront their own fears of the whiteout conditions and the ominous, mysterious drop.

978-1-55469-914-8 pb
978-1-55469-915-5 pdf
978-1-55469-916-2 epub

CASEY FINNEGAN LIVES TO SKATE.

At the end of his final year of high school, Casey is wondering what to do with his life. Other than skateboarding, he doesn't believe he's good at much of anything. When a young movie star contacts Casey and offers him a job as a stunt double in an upcoming skateboarding movie, Casey is stoked. It's his dream job. But when word gets out about Casey's new gig, a local skater has other ideas about who would make the best stunt double. What price will Casey pay to realize his dream?

orca sports

For more information on all the books
in the Orca Sports series, please visit
www.orcabook.com.